THE BEST LAID PLANS

SHAW HART

THE BEST LAID PLANS

 Created with Vellum

*

They say the best laid plans...

Spencer Hayden is lying to himself.

He's been telling himself for years that he doesn't need a family. He doesn't need anyone.

He just got out of the military and he thinks that the freedom to go and do whatever he wants, whenever he wants, is going to make him happy.

The plan is to drive around the country, working the odd job here or there so that he doesn't deplete his savings.

Then he lands in Sunny Bend, Wyoming and meets Emmy Lou Harris.

Emmy Lou is happy with her life.

Sure, she's a little lonely ever since her grandparents died, but she has everything she needs; a good job and friends.

Then Spencer walks into her bookstore and turns her world upside down.

You know what they say about the best laid plans.

They often go awry.

CHAPTER 1

SPENCER

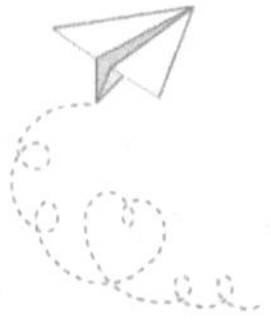

THE PLANE DROWNS out the excited chatter of the skydiving clients that I'm in charge of taking up.

As part of my job at Sunny Side Up Skydiving, I take the newbie skydivers up and partner jump with them. As far as jobs go, it's a pretty good one. I get to skydive all day and the people that I work with are cool. Most of them are ex-military and they all know what they're doing. They're all like me in that regard. I don't think that any of us could handle sitting behind a desk all day or pushing papers around.

I look over to Zac and he gives me a big grin. Jonah is sitting next to him and he flashes me a thumbs up and I nod back, letting him know that I'm good to go. Our pilot, Drew, gives us the signal and Jonah starts to slide his client closer to the plane door.

I just got back from my last deployment and got out of the military a year ago. I had joined right out of high school and spent the last eight years of my life being deployed to different corners of the world.

I was sick of it.

When I first joined, the structure of the military had been great. I needed that then, but after eight years and just as many deployments, I was sick of being told what to do and when to do it. I was sick of being dispatched to war torn countries and leaving feeling like I didn't make a difference. I wanted to be the one to make the plans. I wanted to be in charge of my own life.

When it was time to either re-enlist or get out, I chose to leave. Since then, I promised myself that I would live my life my way. I would have freedom to do what I wanted.

The plan was to drive around the country, working odd jobs to help pay the bills, and never staying in one place for long. I would choose where to stay, where to work, and when to pack up and move on.

So far, the plan is going great. I started in Virginia, drove up to New York but I hated all of the noise and the tourists. It was too crowded so I left and went to Pennsylvania and stayed in Philadelphia and then Pittsburgh. Neither place felt right so I didn't stay for longer than a few weeks.

Since then, I've ping ponged around, from Michigan to Montana, Oregon to California. I spent a crazy few days in Las Vegas before I headed north again and stopped in Wyoming. I had an old Army buddy who lived in Valor, Wyoming now and I stayed with him and his new wife, Bristle, for a few days. Seeing him so settled and happy had me feeling itchy though so it wasn't long before I headed out on the road again.

I just landed in Sunny Bend two weeks ago and I'm hoping to leave in another two. I should have enough money saved by then to make it to the next state and last me a little while.

I don't have a family, no one to spend time or money on. My parents were never real parents, not in any sense of the word. It's why I joined the military right out of high school. It's not like I had any other real options. I never could have afforded college and I didn't want to spend my life working a low level job. So, when the Army recruiter came to my high school, I had been the first one to sign up.

Part of me thought that I would find my family in the Army. I guess all of those recruitment commercials saying that we were an Army of one really got to me.

That wasn't the case for me though. I left the military the way that I entered it. Alone. Although, I did have substantially more money in my bank account and a skill set that could actually lead to better jobs.

I saved most of my money while I was in the military so I have a nice nest egg but I don't want to blow through it too quickly. That's why I'm staying at some cheap rental house in the older, more rundown part of town.

We reach altitude and Jonah slides the door of the plane open. The wind whips inside and sends my hair blowing across my forehead. My heart starts to race, adrenaline flooding my system as I scoot me and my partner up the bench that we're seated on and closer to the door.

"Are you ready?" I yell over the noise and she gives a tentative nod. "It's going to be a blast," I tell her, trying to ease her nerves.

Jonah and his partner go first and I watch them jump. I can feel my partner tense as she watches them jump.

This is usually how it goes. Some people can take it in stride, but most people start to panic as soon as they climb into the plane. By the time that we reach altitude and the plane door opens, they're white as a sheet and I practically have to wrestle them to the door. It's a real cat in the bathtub situation.

Zac and his partner are up next and they jump out the

door, his partner screaming as they go. That definitely isn't going to help my client's nerves. As expected, she tenses up even more, her whole body freezing. I strong-arm us over to the door, noticing how my client's fingers have turned white around the bench seat.

We're last and I look over to Drew, letting him know that the first two jumps went smoothly before we get into position in the open doorway.

"Ready?" I ask. I need to be sure that she really wants to jump.

She gives a shaky nod and I inch us a little closer so we're sitting in the doorway. Our feet are dangling out the open door and I take a deep breath, enjoying the view and the feeling of being right on the edge.

"We're going to count to three and then just fall forward. One, two, three!" I yell, leaning forward and thrusting us out of the plane.

The wind rushes past us and I grin, loving the feeling. We freefall for a few seconds but it's over far too fast. I check the altimeter on my wrist and when it's time, I pull the straps.

The shoot opens, the parachute a bright red cloud above our heads, and we slow. It's so quiet up here and I take a moment to enjoy the peace before I check in with my partner.

"Are you doing alright?" I ask and she nods.

"Yeah," she whispers and I can hear the awe in her voice.

I get it. I still remember the first time I saw the world from five thousand feet up. It makes you feel powerful and yet insignificant at the same time. One thing's for sure, I'd never get the same rush of adrenaline and emotion at a desk job.

The town is spread out below us and I remain quiet for the rest of our descent. When it's time, I tell her to lift her feet up for the landing and we land without incident. She thanks me as I unhook us and I shake her hand before I gather my parachute and head for the staff room.

It looks like rain and I don't think that there will be any more jumps today so I stow all of my gear for tomorrow and get ready to head home. Drew, Zac, and Jonah are all dealing with their own gear and I nod at them as I finish stowing the last of my gear.

"Want to grab drinks with us this weekend?" Jonah asks me, just like every other week.

I know that they're trying to make me feel included and to be friendly, but I never take them up on their offers. I can't get attached here. I know that I'll be leaving soon.

"Thanks, but I have plans. Maybe next time," I say with a wave as I head for the door.

I wave at Colt, my boss and the owner of Sunny Side Up Skydiving as I head for the door.

I stop for food on the way home and have to park a little ways down the block since it's so close to the dinner rush. I head past the pet store, a bookstore, and then the arts and crafts store. I've never been into any of them, no reason to. I know that Jonah has though. He has a thing for the girl, Aurora, who runs the craft store. I think that he's been to every sip and paint class that she's offered. There are a bunch of mugs in the break room at Sunny Side Up Skydiving that he's painted there too. He still hasn't been able to work up the nerve to ask her out though.

I head inside the Sunnyside Bar and Grill and place my to go order. They tell me that it will be half an hour and I pay before I head for the door.

I'm walking back toward my Jeep when the skies open

up and I duck into the first available store. It's a bookstore that's mostly empty and I look around. I'm not even sure that there's anyone working here.

"Hi! Welcome to Book Addicts Bookstore!" Comes a friendly voice and I start, looking over to my right.

There's a shelf there and I spot a woman kneeling behind it. She's got a box of books next to her and is stocking the shelf there.

"Hey," I say, stepping closer to her.

"Welcome! Can I help you find anything in particular?"

"No, I'm just browsing. Trying to escape the rain."

"Oh, I know! It came out of nowhere."

She stands then and heads around the shelf to join me.

My brain short circuits as I get a look at her.

She's gorgeous.

A curtain of rich auburn hair hangs halfway down her back in soft waves. She's wearing black jeans that hug her legs. A loose fitting pale pink t-shirt hides her curves from me but gives me ideas of what she would look like naked and my mouth starts to water.

Her big green eyes sparkle up at me as she gives me a friendly grin and holds out her hand to me.

"I'm Emmy Lou Harris. This is my store," she says.

I slip my hand into hers, marveling over how soft her skin feels.

"I'm Spencer. It's nice to meet you."

My eyes lock on hers and refuse to let go. What is it about this woman? I suddenly want to know everything about her, which could be problematic. I'm not planning on staying here for very long. Certainly not long enough to get attached to anyone or swap life stories. It's never been a problem before, but with Emmy Lou...

She tugs on her hand and I let go of her reluctantly, not

sure what to do about the ache in my chest when she steps away from me.

"I don't think I've seen you around town before," she says as she goes back to finishing stocking the last of the books.

"I just got to town a few weeks ago," I say once I've gotten my crazy thoughts under control. "I'm working over at Sunny Side Up Skydiving."

"You're a skydiving instructor?" She asks, seeming fascinated.

"Yeah," I say, feeling almost proud. I want this girl to find me intriguing. I want her to be just as interested in me as I am in her.

"That's so cool. I've always wanted to do it but it seems so scary. I'm not sure that I'm brave enough."

"It's not so bad. I can take you up if you want to do it sometime."

The idea of her strapped to me has my heart racing and my cock stirring in my jeans.

Normally, I don't pay women too much mind. I'm never really in one place for long and it didn't seem like a good idea to start something with anyone. No one has ever tempted me to change my stance on that.

Until Emmy Lou.

"What are you doing tomorrow night?" I blurt out and she stares up at me wide eyed.

I want to hit myself. I don't want to scare this girl off. I just don't have any practice with all of this. I've never asked a woman out before but it's nice to know that I'm so smooth about it.

"Um, nothing," she says, blushing slightly.

"Have dinner with me."

"Okay," she says shyly and I can't stop the smile from

curving my lips.

The rain stops and I know that my food must be done so I swap phone numbers with her and promise that I'll see her tomorrow before I head out.

My subconscious reminds me that I'm straying from my plan but I shove that voice down. It's just one date.

The plan is still on.

CHAPTER 2

EMMY LOU

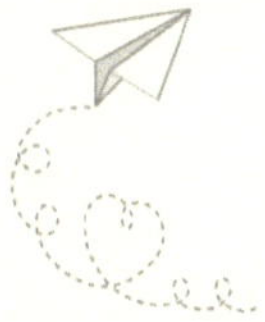

I'VE BEEN out of the dating game for too long.

Actually, I'm not even sure that my one "date" with Robby when we were in kindergarten even really counts. He gave me his apple juice at lunch and then threw glitter at me. All in all, it wasn't the worst way to spend recess.

Something tells me my date with Spencer will more than make up for Robby's unimpressive attempt to get my attention though. He already has all of my attention from just one brief meeting.

Things had been so relaxed last night at the bookstore when we met that it isn't until he's headed to pick me up that I start to get nervous.

I've been texting my best friends, Harlow and Aurora, asking for advice but they haven't been much help. Neither of them date a lot either. Aurora owns the arts and crafts store and Harlow owns the pet store on either side of my bookstore and they saw Spencer coming into my store as they were closing up theirs last night. They had both stopped by after he left and demanded to know all of the details. When I told them that he had asked me out for dinner, they had squealed and happy danced with me.

What am I supposed to wear? Should I have asked him where we were going so that I knew how to dress? What are the rules?

Growing up, the romance parts of fairy tales were always my favorite. I know what people say about me. That I'm naïve and a hopeless romantic, but it's not really my fault.

Growing up, I heard all about the family tradition. For as far back as my grandparents could remember, everyone has taken one look at their future spouse and fallen head over heels in love. There would be this spark, this connection, and you would just know that you had found your other half. Your happily ever after. I can't help but wonder if Spencer is going to be that for me.

Now that it's almost time for Spencer to pick me up, I'm starting to wish that I had asked more questions about the dating part of those stories. In my head, I always pictured a big movie moment where the woman jumped into the arms of her true love and they shared a swoon-worthy kiss in the rain. The details of how exactly they got there didn't interest me, but they sure do now.

Do I hold his hand? Was I supposed to play hard to get when he asked me out last night?

Spencer hadn't seemed put off last night when I had said yes right away. In fact, I would say that he seemed excited about it so I'm guessing I didn't mess that part up at least.

I had been shocked when he asked me out. He was so hot, the most attractive person that I'd ever laid eyes on with his mussed dark brown hair and those piercing blue eyes. When we shook hands, I swear I felt a spark of something between us. His brilliant eyes held mine captive, searching them as if looking for answers. It was intense and a little too much for me, so I had to pull myself away before I did something stupid like kiss him or ask him if he believed in love at first sight like in the fairy tales.

My phone dings and I check the screen, smiling when I see I have a message from Harlow and Aurora, both wishing me well tonight. I'm sure that they'll be calling me tomorrow or stopping by the store to get all of the details.

The doorbell rings and I know that he's here. I make sure that I have my phone and keys in my purse before I cross the room and open the door. Spencer is standing there with a bouquet of flowers and the sight of him takes my breath away.

He's wearing dark blue jeans and a white button-down shirt with the sleeves rolled up. The outfit itself isn't anything special, but the man wearing it... well, let's just say he's filling out those jeans quite nicely. And those fore-arms... good lord.

"Hey," he says with a grin, his blue eyes sparkling at me as he passes me the flowers. So far, this date is already a hundred times better than my "date" with Robby.

"Hey," I say and I start to feel myself relax.

There's something about Spencer that puts me at ease. He seems so laid back and sweet and I feel like I can be myself around him.

I head into the kitchen with the flowers, finding a vase and filling it with water before I arrange the flowers in it.

"Are you ready to go?" He asks and I nod as I grab my purse.

I lock my apartment door behind us and follow him down the front porch steps to his big jeep.

"You look beautiful," he says as he opens the car door for me.

I grin at him as he closes the door and heads around the hood to slide behind the wheel.

Maybe I'm not messing this whole thing up as much as I thought I would.

"Where are we headed?" I ask and he waits until we've merged with traffic before he answers me.

"How do you feel about Italian food?"

"I love it."

"Is Carantino's alright?" He asks me and I nod, giving him a small smile.

Carantino's is a fancy upscale restaurant on the north side of Sunny Bend. I've always wanted to try it but I never had a reason to go or anyone to go with. Until now.

"Sounds perfect. I've never been there but I've heard good things."

I ask him about the skydiving today and how he got into that line of work as we drive.

"I was in the military. Army and then I became a Ranger. I just got out last year actually," he says and the short haircut clicks.

It's done in the traditional military style. Him being in the Army also fits with him. He seems like a good guy, a protector. He's capable and strong.

He parks at the restaurant and leads me inside Carantino's. The place is done in deep reds and blacks. It's an intimate setting with a candle on each of the small tables that are situated around the space.

We're led to a table in the back and I wait until we've placed our drink orders before I start a new conversation.

"How are you liking Sunny Bend so far?" I ask and he smiles.

"It's a cool little town. It's been a real change from being deployed overseas or on a military base. I think I'm still getting adjusted," he admits and I nod.

"I'm sure you'll get the hang of things soon," I reassure him.

"Me too," he says, giving me a grin.

"Were you deployed a lot?" I ask him as our drinks are set down.

"Yeah, I was on a cycle so I would be in the states for six months and then overseas for six months. Sometimes longer if they ended up dispatching my unit somewhere else."

"Did you like it?" I ask quietly, afraid that I'm prying too much.

I couldn't imagine moving around like that, from one extreme to the other, but maybe he likes it. It's fascinating and so different from the life I've led.

"At first I did. Over time it got old though. That's why I got out."

The waitress comes back and drops off some bread and I thank her as I grab a piece.

"What about you? When did you open Book Addicts Bookstore?"

"I've always loved to read and when the old owner was ready to retire, she sold it to me."

"Sounds like you lucked out," he says with a warm smile, taking a bite of his own piece of bread.

"I did," I say.

The conversation turns to our pasts and I tell him about growing up in Sunny Bend with my grandparents. My parents passed when I was a teenager and I lived with them until I went away to college.

I had just graduated and moved back to Sunny Bend

when they passed. They left me their house and some money and that's how I was able to buy the bookstore.

He doesn't really mention his parents and I can tell that it's a sensitive subject for him. I don't want to pry. It doesn't feel appropriate on our first date. He just makes some disparaging comment about deadbeat parents and I leave it at that. Maybe I'll get him to open up to me more later on.

He fills me in on some of his deployments and the bases that he's been stationed at over the years. I'm enthralled by his stories and how many places he's been to. I've always wanted to travel but never found the time or the money so it's nice to live vicariously through him.

The waiter comes back and we place our orders. The next two hours seem to pass by in a flash and before I know it, he's paying the bill and we're headed outside to his car.

"Thanks for dinner," I say as I step closer to his side on the sidewalk.

"It was my pleasure," he says, wrapping his arm around my waist as he leads me to his Jeep.

He opens my door for me again and we talk more about places that we've been and want to go as he drives me back to my place. It's already getting pretty late by the time that we pull up to my front door.

"I had a lot of fun tonight," I say softly and he turns the car off and turns to face me.

"Me too."

The air crackles and sparks between us, tension building with each passing second. I'm not sure what the protocol is here. Do I have to wait until he walks me to my front door to ask for a kiss? What if I want one now?

We both move at the same time and our lips collide, fusing together as his hands get tangled in my hair. I tug him closer and he goes eagerly, his hand cupping the back of my head as I open under him and he slips his tongue inside my mouth.

He tastes like the coffee and chocolate tiramisu that we split for dessert and I moan, wanting to eat him instead.

Before I can put that plan into motion, we're cut off. His phone rings, breaking into my thoughts and we pull back, breathing hard.

I stare at him, trying to reign in my libido as I reach for the door handle. His phone is still ringing and he tries to stop me but I open the door.

"I'll let you get that. Call me later," I say, leaning over and brushing a kiss across his lips before I slide out of the car.

I wish that he could walk me up to my door, but the phone call interrupting us is probably for the best. I'm not sure that I can pull myself from going all of the way with him tonight and I don't want this to just be about sex.

He waits while I walk up the stairs and let myself inside. I give him a wave as he starts up his Jeep and heads down the road.

My body is still buzzing as I put on my pajamas and slide into bed and I smile as I close my eyes.

It feels like I might have finally found my Prince Charming and I can already see Spencer being my happily ever after.

I let those thoughts follow me into my dreams.

CHAPTER 3

SPENCER

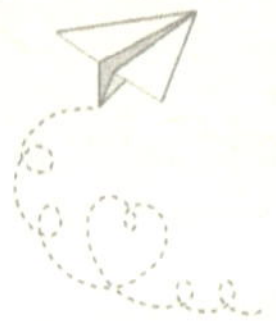

I HAVEN'T BEEN able to stop thinking about Emmy Lou since last night. Even today when I was at work, she found a way to wiggle into my thoughts and distract me.

I nearly groan just thinking about that kiss. I had wanted to kiss her ever since I picked her up for our date last night. She looked like a vision.

The light green dress she was wearing hugged her curves and matched her beautiful green eyes. Her full, pouty lips called to me all night. It was the sweetest kind of torture to watch her wrap those lips around her fork while we shared a slice of tiramisu. My cock jerked in my damn jeans when she licked a few crumbs off of her bottom lip.

I was going crazy by the time I loaded her up in my car and drove her back to her place, but I didn't want to push her into anything or pressure her for more. Good thing Emmy Lou wanted me as much as I wanted her. I'm not sure who initiated the kiss, only that it was incredible. Dangerous. Addicting.

It was Colt who called me last night, breaking our kiss. He had wanted to know if I could fill in for Jonah today and

I had told him I could and tried not to be pissed at him for interrupting Emmy Lou and I.

Today was pretty slow and Zac and I were easily able to handle all of the clients that came in. It was so slow that Drew even took Zac and I up alone so that we could jump solo. It's been a while since I've been able to do that.

When it's time for me to clock out, I know that I should head home but I find myself swinging down Main Street and pulling into a spot in front of her bookstore.

I can see her moving around inside, helping a customer and I smile. There are two other girls inside and they look familiar. I must have seen them around town somewhere.

She's got her hair tied up into a high ponytail today and is wearing a flowy spaghetti strap dress with polka dots all over it. She's a ray of sunshine, optimism shining from every pore. It's so unlike anyone that I've ever known. Maybe that's why I'm so addicted to her.

It's got to be close to closing time for her so I get out of my Jeep and head inside. The other customer is leaving and Emmy Lou turns to me with a bright smile as I head up to the checkout counter. The other two women look on with curiosity and excitement in their eyes.

"We'll leave you two alone, Emmy Lou," one of the women says.

"Yeah, we'll see you tomorrow!" The other says and Emmy Lou gives them a smile over her shoulder.

"Have a good night guys!"

"Hey," I say once we're alone.

"Hey, what are you doing here?" She asks me as she comes around the counter.

"I wanted to see you. Are you closing soon?"

"Yeah, right now actually."

"Can I take you out to dinner again?" I ask and she nods.

"I'd like that."

It doesn't take her long to close down and I wait while she locks the front door and tucks her keys in her purse before I take her hand and lead her over to my Jeep.

"What would you like to eat?" I ask her and she bites her lip.

"How about Lulu's Diner? They've got a bunch of options and their food is good."

I nod, steering us in that direction as I ask her about her day. She tells me about some new romance books that she just got in that she's excited about and her excitement has a knot forming in my stomach.

I can feel myself starting to lose sight of my plan as she goes on. She's obviously a romantic at heart and I should back off. I can't seem to force myself to stop asking her out or wanting to spend time with her though.

We pull up to Lulu's Diner and I help her out. We find a booth and she smiles happily as she looks over the menu. Lulu's is a 50's style diner in the center of town. According to the back of the menu, it's been a part of this town since the eighties and has some of the best food in the area. I've only been here once so while it's obvious that although it's in desperate need of a remodel and some updates, the food really is some of the best in town.

Our waitress comes over and neither one of us bothers to look at the menu. We both order the burgers and fries and a milkshake and then relax against the booth.

"How was your day?" She asks me and I tell her about the big, tough acting dude who had fainted as soon as we jumped out of the plane and then tried to play it off like it didn't happen once we landed.

Emmy Lou giggles, loving me re-enacting him fainting against my chest as we fell back to Earth. I tell her how his friends had been teasing him before we could even get the parachute off. I doubt that he'll be trying skydiving again. Not anytime soon at least.

I have a few more stories like that from other clients of the past or from people that I was in bootcamp with who had flunked out.

We laugh and tell funny stories throughout our meal. I love getting to know Emmy Lou more. She sounds like she's always been an optimist, always cheerful, even when she lost her parents or was picked on in school. It's a foreign concept. To not take everything so personally. To not let others actions get to you or to just let things go.

I pay the bill when it comes and leads her back out to my Jeep. It's starting to drizzle so I take off my jacket and hold it over our heads as we jog across the parking lot to where I'm parked.

I don't really want to take her home and have our date be over just yet but I know that we both have early mornings.

We hold hands as I drive down the streets back to her place. I drive slower, blaming it on the rain, but I know that the real reason is because I don't want this night to be over just yet.

When we pull up out front, she unbuckles and then leans over the console and we go from zero to one hundred in the blink of an eye.

Her mouth tastes like the salt from the fries and chocolate from her milkshake and I moan, pulling her closer. She crawls into my lap at the same time that I push my seat back and I tug her closer to me.

Her curves mold against my hard body and she starts to

rock against the ridge of my cock. My jeans are strangling my cock but I'm not about to stop her. Not with her moaning and grinding down on top of me.

"Spencer," she purrs and I kiss her hard, trying to stamp my claim on her.

"That's it, baby. Show me how you get off."

That's all it takes and she gasps, her fingers digging into my shoulders as her eyes go blank with bliss and she squirms on top of me.

"Spencer," she breathes against my lips and my heart stops in my chest.

Right then and there, that's when it happens.

That's when I start to fall for Emmy Lou Harris and I don't think that I'll be able to stop it from happening.

I don't think that I want to.

CHAPTER 4

EMMY LOU

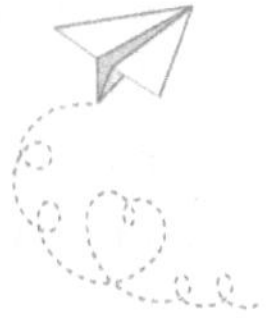

MY BODY HAS BEEN BUZZING like I was plugged into a socket since last night. I've touched myself and made myself come before but never like that. It's never been that intense or lasted as long as it did last night when I was moving on top of Spencer.

He had felt so powerful beneath me. So strong and sexy. And his words, Jesus, his words are what sent me flying over the edge.

We're going out again tonight and I can't wait. I want to see him again. I want to go all of the way with him.

That thought has me nervous but also excited. I don't know what it is about Spencer, but it feels like he's meant to be mine.

My grandparents told me that love at first sight runs in our family. My grandma and grandpa knew that they were meant to be as soon as they're eyes met across a crowded diner. It was the same way for my mom and dad. They were at summer camp and my mom walked out of her cabin and looked up. They were together until they passed.

I wonder if Spencer can feel this between us too or if it's

just me. I don't think he would keep asking me out if he didn't feel something for me.

The doorbell rings and I straighten my tight dress as I cross the room and answer the door.

"Hey," I say when he just stands there and stares at me.

"Emmy Lou, you look... wow," he finishes in awe and I feel my whole body warm at his praise.

I told him that I would make dinner for us here and I close the door after him before I give him the tour of my small bungalow style house.

"It smells good in here," he compliments me as we walk into the kitchen and I laugh.

"It's nothing fancy. Roasted chicken and vegetables."

"Sounds perfect. I haven't had a home cooked meal in a while."

I pour each of us a glass of wine and we sit at the counter waiting for the food to be done. He asks me about some of the pictures on the walls and I tell him more about my parents and grandparents.

He laughs when I tell him about going to Six Flags for vacation one year. I threw up on almost every ride I went on and have refused to set foot on a rollercoaster since.

He tells me that he almost fainted once in bootcamp and that he threw up the first day of Ranger school.

The oven timer goes off and I grab the food out of the oven as Spencer starts to grab us plates and silverware. We work together seamlessly and a vision of us doing this every night flits through my mind.

It sounds perfect but I keep that to myself as we each make a plate and head back to the barstools at the counter.

We talk while we eat. I tell him about growing up here in Sunny Bend and some of my favorite books. I mention one that he saw as a movie and when he mentions that, I jump into a spirited argument of all the ways the movie was different from the book and all the reasons that the book was better.

Spencer watches me the entire time, hanging on my every word and looking at me like I'm the most adorable thing that he's ever seen. It's nice to see that my passion for books isn't weird to him.

I ask him more about himself and he seems like he's trying to keep it light. I wonder if he just doesn't want to bring up his parents which only makes me wonder more about his childhood and family life.

The weather was bad today so he only went up once before they were grounded. He doesn't seem that upset by it and I wonder if skydiving gets old after a while.

After dinner, he helps me do dishes and the closer we stand together, the more he brushes against me as he puts the plates and silverware away, the higher the sexual tension climbs.

"Emmy Lou," Spencer whispers as his arms bracket my waist and he pushes me back against the counter.

I lick my lips, startled by the desire that I can see burning in his eyes.

"I want you," I murmur and that's all it takes.

His lips land on mine.

The kiss starts off hot and heavy, both of us desperate for the contact and probably praying that the other doesn't change their mind. One taste of him though, and I can't pull away.

He grabs my hips, dragging me closer to him and I go happily. My fingers are tugging at the button of his jeans. I can feel his cock pushing against the front of them, trying its best to get closer to me.

"Bedroom?" He rasps out against my lips and I grab his hand, leading him down the hallway.

I turn on the lamp by my bedside and then turn back to him. His hands go to the zipper of my dress and he tugs it down. He helps me wiggle out of it and then I'm reaching for his clothes.

He's all too happy to help me strip him out of his jeans and shirt and together we pull off the last of our clothes.

I wrap my arms around his neck as he topples us over onto the mattress. I should probably be self-conscious since this is the first time that I've been naked in front of someone, but I'm too focused on the things Spencer is making me feel.

His body is strong, like a wall of muscle against mine and I moan as his calloused hands run over me.

"Spencer," I moan, my legs spreading of their own free will as he moves between them.

He kisses down my neck and takes one sweet tip into his mouth, sucking hard. An answering tingle starts between my legs and my fingers tangle in his hair, holding him closer to me.

He teases my sweet peaks for another minute before he kisses lower, over the soft swell of my stomach and lower.

"You're so fucking pretty, baby. So fucking gorgeous," he groans against my skin.

My legs start to quiver as he settles between them and reaches up, spreading my wet pussy lips.

"Oh, baby. You're absolutely drenched for me already," he says, his voice low and husky.

That tone of voice has tingles racing down my spine and I let out a sharp gasp, my hips shooting off of the bed in a wordless plea as he rolls his thumb over my sensitive clit.

He doesn't make me beg for long before he buries his face in my soft pink folds. He eats me like a man starved, licking and nipping at my core. His tongue plunges into my tight little hole and he fucks me with it as his thumb strokes over my clit until I'm a shaking, moaning, panting mess.

"Spencer!" I cry out and he licks me faster.

"I want you to come for me, baby. Give it to me," he orders, running his fingers up my slit.

I cry out, my fingers gripping the short strands of his hair tighter as he thrusts one thick digit into my opening.

He licks a path right up my center, his tongue doing lazy circles around my clit and that's all it takes to have me sailing over the edge.

"Spencer!" I shout as I come against his mouth.

"That's it, baby. Are you ready for me?" He asks, kissing his way back up my body and I nod wordlessly.

He reaches down between us, fisting his cock as he guides it to my wet entrance. He kisses me and I can taste myself on his mouth.

I moan, twisting my tongue with his as he starts to work his cock into my tight channel.

"Please," I beg, spreading my legs wider as he pushes the rest of the way inside of me and pops my cherry.

He gives me a minute to adjust but soon I'm squirming under him, trying to get him to move.

Spencer seems to get the message because he starts a slow, even pace that drives me out of my mind in no time.

"Oh, god," I moan, my eyes falling closed as his cock drags over this amazing spot deep inside of me.

"Emmy Lou," he grits out and goosebumps break out on my skin.

His hands grip around my upper thighs and he kneels between my legs, moving me up higher so that the root of his big dick can brush over my clit with each pass.

My whole body is coiling tighter and tighter with each

pass and before I know it, my orgasm is bearing down on me again.

"I'm going to come," I gasp and he picks up his pass.

"Do it, baby. I want to see it. I want to feel you come all over my cock."

Just like that, I'm flying.

I can hear him grunt out my name as his own release hits me and then we're rolling until I'm sprawled out on top of him.

"Wow," I whisper and he grunts out his agreement.

His hands stroke up and down my back and I let my eyes drift shut as I relax against him.

I fall asleep with a smile on my face.

CHAPTER 5

SPENCER

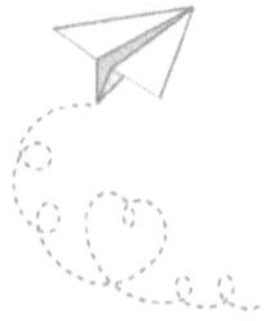

I'M SCREWED.

It's only been a few days but I can already feel myself sinking further and further into Emmy Lou.

How could anyone not love her? Not that I'm in love with her, but I could see how someone could be. She's sweet and smart. She makes me laugh and for the first time in a really long while, it feels like someone in the world actually cares about me.

I haven't had that before. My parents were both addicts who forgot that I existed most of the time and the military liked to thank me for my service but as soon as I was out, I was dropped like a bad habit.

Emmy Lou is loyal though. She wouldn't just leave me. Not unless I gave her a reason.

I'm at war. My head is telling me to stick to the plan, to get that freedom that I wanted for so long, but my heart says otherwise. It says that I'm never going to find another girl as perfect as Emmy Lou and I shouldn't waste this chance. I should pick her.

My heart is winning and that's a problem.

Even when I'm panicking about my feelings for her though, I can't seem to stop myself from searching her out. That's why I'm headed down Main Street toward the Book Addicts Bookstore.

It's close to closing time and I'm hoping that I can catch her before she goes home. Maybe I can take her out to dinner again.

I park and see her headed for the front door, her purse and keys in her hand and I hop out.

"Hey, I was hoping to catch you," I say as I step inside the bookstore and she looks up and spots me.

She beams at me, her whole face lighting up and it causes my heart to seize up in my chest. The things this girl does to me.

"Hey, I was just about to text you," she says as she leans up on her tiptoes and kisses me.

It's over way too fast and she must agree too because her eyes lock with mine and she wraps her arms around my neck.

The kiss starts off soft and sweet, both of us in no rush. I want to explore every inch of her, to take my time this time. One taste of her though, and I can't pull away. The longer we kiss, the deeper I feel myself sink into her. Soon it's like I can't get close enough to her, and she seems to feel the same way about me.

I grab Emmy Lou's hip, dragging her closer to me as I back her up, headed toward the comfy looking couch along the back wall of the bookstore.

Her little fingers are tugging at my pants and I can feel my cock growing with each twitch of her hand against my length. I let go of her waist, helping her unbutton my pants and push them down before I kick them and my shoes off the rest of the way.

My hands reach for her dress right away and together we work on pulling it off over her head and tossing it to the floor with my clothes.

Her perky breasts bounce slightly as she unhooks her bra and lets it join the rest of our clothes on the floor as she follows me over to the couch. We both reach for our underwear at the same time and then she's pushing me down on the couch and straddling me.

My hands cup her breasts and I tweak the stiff peaks between my fingers as she starts to grind on top of me. They're a perfect handful and I can't wait to get my mouth on them again.

"Oh, Spencer," Emmy Lou moans, her eyes falling to half-mast as I roll her stiff nipples between my fingers.

I tease the sweet peaks, watching as a blush creeps over her whole body. Soon, I can't take it any longer and I roll us over on the couch so that she's beneath me. I hover over her, kissing a path down to one soft swell.

"You're so fucking perfect, Emmy Lou," I groan as I lean down and capture one of her nipples in my mouth.

I look up, watching as she opens her mouth, sucking in a breath as I roll my tongue over one sensitive point and then the other. I take my time exploring her and by the time I've released her breasts, her nipples are red and wet from my mouth and we're both hungry for more.

Her hands tangle in my hair as I lick a path straight down to her core. She spreads her thighs wide for me and I look up to see that her eyes are locked on me and the dark blue depths look bottomless.

Her legs start to quiver as I settle between them and reach up, spreading her dewy pussy lips.

She's drenched and my mouth waters and I lick my lips, wanting to taste her sweet juices again. I can't resist any longer so I lean forward, burying my face in her soft pink folds as I start to lick. She tastes like honey and now I'm the one moaning. I plunge my tongue into her tight little hole and fuck her with it as my thumb strokes over her clit until she's a shaking, moaning, mess.

"Spencer!" she cries out and I pull away to watch her face for a moment.

"That's it," I say, running my finger up her center.

She makes a high-pitched whining sound and it's music to my ears. I lick a path right up her center, my tongue doing lazy circles around her clit. Emmy Lou's hips start to move with me and I smile against her skin.

"I know what you need, baby," I promise her.

My tongue finds her clit again and I push down on the sensitive button, wiggling my tongue slightly side to side until Emmy Lou's legs clamp down like a vise around my head. She moans, her fingers abandoning my hair to try to find purchase on the couch cushions instead.

I add my fingers as I work to push her over the edge. I slip one long finger inside of her, curling it to rub against her front wall and she stiffens, her whole body freezing as her orgasm hits her.

"That's it, baby," I whisper as I continue to lick her through her release.

Her body relaxes as I crawl up her body, bracing myself on the couch above her.

"I want you," she says, her eyes heavy lidded and filled with lust as she stares up at me.

I give her a grin and line my cock up with her snug opening. She's still so tight, even after last night, and I worry that I'm hurting her so I try to distract her, tonguing her nipples, loving them with my mouth as I fit the tip of my cock into her snug hole. I lick and suck while I work my dick into her tight channel.

She's already clamping down around me and I know that neither of us are going to last long.

"You feel so fucking good," I grit out and she moans, arching under me.

"Right there!" She cries and my pace grows erratic as she starts to find her peak.

"Fuck, Emmy Lou," I gasp as she comes around my cock, massaging my own release from me as she goes over the edge.

I collapse on top of her but quickly move so that we're laying on our sides, facing each other.

She sighs and I scoot closer, wanting to make sure that she's warm enough and she nuzzles into me.

"I love you, Spencer," she says dreamily and my body freezes.

She cuddles closer to me, drifting off to sleep and I lay there staring at the ceiling, wondering if I'm about to make the worst decision of my life.

CHAPTER 6
EMMY LOU

IT'S BEEN close to a week since Spencer and I had sex in my store and I told him that I love him. I had fallen asleep pretty fast after that but I still remember that he hadn't said anything back.

And now he's acting strange.

He's stopped by the bookstore twice in the last week and both times he's acted weird. He seems off. Instead of teasing me or being the sweet guy that I've gotten to know over the last few weeks, he's quiet and withdrawn.

He hasn't tried to sleep with me either. He just kisses me goodnight before he leaves. Their chaste kisses, barely there before he pulls away and gives me a forced smile and leaves.

He's stopped stopping by every night, stopped texting and calling me every day and it's been taking him longer and longer to get back to me when I text him. He keeps telling me that he's tired but I don't believe it.

Now I haven't heard from him in over two days.

I can't figure out what happened, why he's acting like this.

I've tried to talk to Harlow and Aurora about it, but they don't have any answers either. I know that they're both just as shocked as me at him going cold all of a sudden. They've tried to support me over the last few days but it's getting to be too much.

Did I do something wrong?

That's the one thought that I can't seem to shake.

I should have waited until he said it first or maybe until we knew each other a little better or longer. I didn't want to wait though. I don't want to wait or hold back with him.

I still can't believe that he hasn't reached out to me though. I didn't think that he was that type of man.

My heart aches and I look at the clock. No one has come into the store for the past hour and it's only another hour until closing time so I decide to leave early. I need to go home and drown my sorrows in some wine and ice cream.

I lock up and climb behind the wheel of my car but as I pull out of my parking spot, I make a decision.

Spencer told me that he was renting some house over on 19th Street and I know the one that he was talking about. Before I can talk myself out of it, I head in that direction.

I pull up out front before I even have a chance to figure out what I'm going to say to him. Do I just demand to know why he hasn't reached out to me? Do I ask if I did something wrong the other night?

Spencer is outside loading a duffle bag into the back of his Jeep and my heart cracks at the sight. *Is he leaving?*

"Spencer," I say as I climb out of my car and walk up behind him.

His back tenses and he takes a deep breath before he turns to face me.

"Emmy Lou. What are you doing here?" He asks.

"I came to see why you hadn't called me."

"I've been tired," he says and I am so sick of hearing that lame excuse.

"Really," I deadpan and I swear I see him flinch.

"And I've just been really busy with work."

I can tell that he's lying and that knowledge cuts deep. He won't make eye contact with me and I don't know how we got to this point. How did everything between us go so wrong?

"Are you going somewhere?" I ask, eyeing the luggage in the back of his Jeep.

"I..."

The one word hangs in the air between us and I swallow hard. This is the end. I can feel it. Tears well in my eyes even as red hot anger fills me.

I ball my hands into fists, digging my nails into my palms to try to stem the tears that I can feel threatening to spill over. I don't want to cry in front of him. I don't want to show him how much he's hurting me.

"I have a right to know. Why have you been acting so distant ever since we slept together in the bookstore? Are you going somewhere?"

"Emmy Lou," he says softly and my heart cracks open the rest of the way. "I was never going to stay in Sunny Bend for long. I don't want to stay anywhere for long. My plan was always to leave."

"I..." I choke out the one word before the first tear slips free.

Dammit, Emmy Lou. Keep it together! You're stronger than this.

"Emmy Lou. Please, baby."

"Don't call me baby," I say, my voice hard and thick with my unshed tears.

"I'm sorry. Please don't cry. I care for you, I do, but I have to leave. The plan was always for me to leave."

"Then why did you get involved with me? Why ask me out? Why spend all of this time getting to know me if you were just going to leave? If you knew that you were always going to leave me? Was I just a fling?"

More tears slip free but I don't care. My whole body is starting to grow numb and I welcome the feeling. Anything is better than feeling my heart being ripped out and stomped on.

"I... I couldn't help myself. Not with you. I know that I should have told you sooner and I'm sorry."

"Right," I say, backing up to my car. "I get it. I'm not worth sticking around for or telling the truth to. Good luck on your trip."

I can tell that I'm about to really start sobbing and I want to keep some of my dignity intact. I can't do that if I ugly cry in front of him.

"Emmy Lou, wait. It's not like that," he says as he takes a step towards me but I hold my hands out. I don't want him to try to comfort me right now.

"Right."

"Emmy Lou, I mean it. It's not you."

"Oh my god! Don't you dare say the it's not you, it's me speech!"

"It's true, Emmy Lou. I just spent the last eight years of my life in the military, being told what to do and when to do it. I'm sick of being dispatched to wherever in the world they decide they need me. I want freedom and to choose where I go."

"I got it, Spencer. It's just that you should have told me that before you asked me out. You don't think that I deserved the choice of starting something with you if I knew you were just going to ditch me? You don't think that would be something that I wanted to know before you took my virginity? Before I fell for you?"

His mouth opens but no words come out. At least he looks ashamed of himself but it does little to ease my pain.

"Enjoy your freedom."

My voice cracks on the last few words and I turn from him and jog back to my car.

"Emmy Lou!" He calls after me but I'm already slamming the door and pulling away from his house and from him.

Unfortunately, the hurt still follows me.

The tears start to fall and I have to slow down so that I can see the road clearly. I park haphazardly in the driveway and rush inside, slamming and locking the door after me.

I don't think that he'll come after me, but if he does, I don't want to see him.

He broke my heart. He crushed all of the dreams that I was already building in my head for our future.

As I curl up on my bed and sob, one thought sticks with me.

I guess the love at first sight family tradition skips a generation.

CHAPTER 7

SPENCER

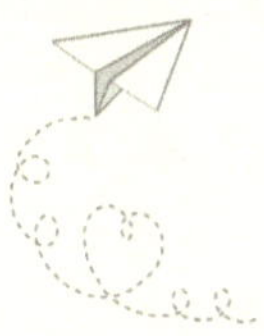

EMMY LOU'S tear-stained face is burned into my brain. It's the first thing I think about when I wake up in the morning and the last image that haunts me as I drift off into a restless sleep at night.

Hell, every time I blink, I see her red-rimmed eyes and quivering bottom lip. The spark in her green eyes flickered and then went out completely when I told her I was always planning to leave. It's true, but then why did the words taste like battery acid on my tongue?

I had thought that it would be easier to just disappear instead of having a long, drawn-out goodbye, but it's been close to a week and with every mile that passes between me and her, the ache in my chest only grows bigger and bigger.

I've tried to fight it, to ignore it, but it just keeps spreading until my whole body feels like an exposed nerve. I ruined my ray of sunshine.

I left Sunny Bend and came back to Valor, Wyoming. Wild had taken one look at my face when I showed up on his doorstep last night and told me that he would make up the guest bed. He let me sulk around his house all day yesterday, but it looks like his patience has worn thin.

"Alright, what's going on with you?" Wild asks as he takes a seat on the couch next to me.

"I met someone."

His eyes widen comically and I roll my own.

"Whoa. Who's the lucky girl?" He asks.

"Her name is Emmy Lou."

"Congrats, man."

"I fucked it up," I admit.

"Yeah, I figured that part out because you're here on my couch instead of with her. What happened?"

I break and pour it all out to him. My plan to travel and make my own way and my own rules. Landing in Sunny Bend a few weeks ago and working at Sunny Side Up Skydiving. Meeting Emmy Lou. I tell him all of it.

At the end, he stares at me for a beat and then smacks me upside the head.

"What the hell?"

"So, you had a girl that you obviously care a lot for, and who likes you back, and you left because of some plan?

I cross my arms over my chest, knowing that he's about to tell me that I'm the biggest idiot that he knows.

"Plans change, Spencer. You can't plan everything. You think I planned to fall in love with Bristle?"

I look over to where his wife is making dinner in the kitchen.

"I didn't, because you can't plan that. It just happened and I thank god every single day that it did. If you feel a fraction of what I feel for Bristle, for Emmy Lou, then you need to go back and make things right."

With that, he stands and heads over to help his wife. He wraps his arms around her waist and she smiles. Things seem so easy between them and it reminds me of how things were with Emmy Lou and I.

That was two days ago.

I've come to realize that Wild was right. My plan of sneaking out might have been easier for me to deal with than my terrifying feelings, but it was ultimately cowardly. I'm ashamed of my actions, or lack thereof. That's not who I am. That's not what eight years in the military taught me.

Meeting her changed my plans, so what? Why was it so important for me to travel the country and gather up new experiences when the only thing I truly want to experience is life with Emmy Lou?

I've been driving all night to make it back to her and I just made it to the next state over. I should be able to make it back to Sunny Bend in time to catch her after closing tomorrow night.

I just stopped for gas and something to eat and I know that I should get a motel room for the night. I'm exhausted but I'd rather get back to Emmy Lou then waste time sleeping.

I thought that I wanted freedom, that constantly moving and being alone would make me happy, but I'm realizing that I was wrong.

I was trying to protect myself. I thought that by pushing people away, they would never be able to hurt me, but Emmy Lou made it past my defenses.

Part of me knows that Emmy Lou would never just leave me, which means that I don't need to be alone to be happy. I just need Emmy Lou.

God, I'm such an idiot.

I'm in love with Emmy Lou and instead of holding onto her and being thankful that I found someone who wants me and loves me, I acted like a scared little boy and pushed her away.

I need Emmy Lou. She makes me see the good in other people, in the world.

I don't want freedom. Not if it means that I lose Emmy Lou in the process.

I'm exhausted and I know that it will take me another eighteen hours to make it back to Sunny Bend, but that doesn't deter me from climbing back behind the wheel and heading back toward town and my girl.

I just hope that it's not too late for me to make things right with my girl.

I spend the whole drive back to Sunny Bend trying to come up with a plan. I'm going to have to grovel, to apologize and try to win her back but when I pull up outside of the Book Addicts Bookstore, I still don't have anything figured out.

I fucked up. I fucked up bad.

She's starting to close up when I walk inside. I try to show her how apologetic that I am as I approach her but she just glares at me. I can see the anger and hurt swirling in her eyes and I know that I deserve her wrath.

"Hey," I try and she just folds her arms over her chest.

Her eyes are a little swollen and red rimmed and I know that she's been crying. Dammit. It's the same broken-hearted, vulnerable look she had the last time I saw her, but there's more than a little anger there as well. That's alright. I'm willing to do whatever it takes to make her trust me, make her love me. I swallow hard and take a step closer to her.

"I'm sorry."

"Not good enough," she snaps and I nod.

I know that she's right.

She pushes past me, flipping off the lights as she grabs her purse and heads for the front door. I hurry after her.

"Emmy Lou, please. Let me apologize. Let me try to explain."

She scoffs and my heart cracks a little more.

"I messed up, Emmy Lou. I know that. I just got scared. I'm not used to people caring for me."

"If you get scared then you talk to people. You don't run away," she throws over her shoulder.

"I know. I'm sorry. I don't have many, or any, examples of a healthy relationship. Remember when you asked me about my parents?"

She nods, pausing as she fiddles with her keys.

"Well the truth is that they were both deadbeats. They were addicts who spent all of their time and money chasing their vices. They barely even remembered that they had a kid most days."

"I'm sorry, Spencer. I truly am. I can't imagine what that would be like... but that doesn't excuse how you hurt me. I can't just forgive you after you were going to leave without even saying goodbye."

"I know, but if you just give me a second chance, I promise that it will never happen again."

She swallows hard and looks away from me.

"I thought you were one of the good guys," she whispers. Her soft voice cuts deeper than yelling and screaming ever could. "You walked away from me, after I told you that I love you. You're the only guy I've ever said that to. Didn't it mean something? Didn't *I* mean something? And you just left without a second thought. What's to stop you from doing it again?"

My mouth opens but I don't know how to reassure her. Instead I follow after her out onto the sidewalk and wait as she locks the front door. I feel like even more of an ass. Not only did I break her heart, but I turned into the very thing I hate; someone who abandons and hurts the ones they love. It kills me to know I caused the same pain in her heart that I've always felt deep in mine.

"I love you, Emmy Lou," I whisper and she shakes her head as she walks past me.

"I'm sorry, but I don't believe you," she says as she opens her car door.

"Then I'll prove it to you," I vow.

She stares at me for a beat before she slams the car door closed and pulls away from me.

Well, that could have gone better but there's still a chance that I can turn this around.

I just need to show her that I'm never going to make the mistake of leaving her again.

CHAPTER 8

EMMY LOU

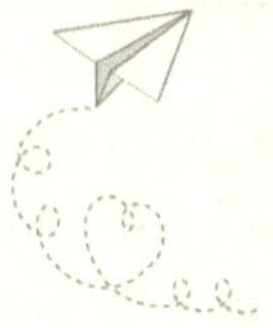

I DON'T KNOW what to think about Spencer showing up here last night after a week of nothing. Part of me had been happy to see him but then everything that happened between us hit me and all I felt was rage.

It was too little, too late.

His apology had seemed sincere but I can't give into him. Not if he's just going to leave me again. I barely survived it the first time. There's no way I'd make it if he left me a second time.

I keep thinking about the family legend. That I would just find someone, take one look at him, and know that he was meant to be mine. I thought that I had found that with Spencer, but obviously, I was wrong. How can I trust my own judgment in the future?

I just need to give up my ideas of finding my Prince Charming and getting my happily ever after.

My heart aches at the thought but it's hurt a lot more since Spencer walked away without a backward glance. I spent the last week walking around like a zombie. I barely ate anything. I wasn't hungry and every time I tried to force myself to grab something to eat, it only reminded me of us going out to eat together.

Everything seemed to remind me of him. Driving past LuLu's, seeing a Jeep or a plane, hell, even being in my own store.

I spent most of the time that I wasn't at work curled up in my bed crying until I fell asleep. Harlow and Aurora both did everything that they could to be there for me and to try to cheer me up but I just wanted to be alone. I felt too raw to be around other people. That didn't stop them from checking on me and I know that I'm lucky to have such great friends.

I spent most of my time at home. I could barely stand to be at the bookstore. Every time the door opened, I found myself wishing that it was him and I couldn't look at the couch in the back without picturing the two of us making love there, before everything fell apart.

I've been miserable without him but I'm sure that it will pass soon. I just need time to heal. That's why it's better if I just push him away now. I'm sure that he'll get tired of chasing me soon and move on. I just need to stay strong until then.

It's almost closing time when the door opens and I know without looking that it's Spencer.

I steel my walls, taking a deep breath before I turn to face him.

"Hey, I brought you some dinner," he says with a hopeful smile and I can feel myself starting to melt.

I straighten my shoulders and give him my sternest look.

"You didn't have to do that."

"I wanted to," he says, setting the bag of takeout on the counter.

"Why?" I snap.

All of my anger comes out in that one word and I can't tell if Spencer is shocked or if this is what he expected to happen eventually.

"Why do you want to bring me food? You pushed me away. You left for a week without looking back. If you want your freedom so badly, then you should leave."

"I don't want freedom, Emmy Lou. I was wrong. I just want you. I need you."

I look away from him, pacing a few feet away.

"I know that you don't trust me. I know that I'll have to earn your trust back, earn your love back and I'm willing to do whatever it takes to win you back. I know you don't believe me right now, but I love you Emmy Lou. I don't want my freedom. I want you. I want a family."

His voice cracks on the last word and I stare down at my feet. His words hit me deep, especially after he told me about his parents. He's been hurt, too, but he genuinely wants to have his own family, to try and be a better parent than either of his were.

I steel my resolve, however. It's all well and good that he realized he wants to settle down, but I'm not ready to give up my anger just yet.

We stand in silence for long moments until he breaks it.

"I started looking for a house in town," he blurts out.

His words from last night hit me. He's going to prove that he's not going to leave me again and this is his way of showing that he's not going anywhere.

"I found a few that are close to downtown," he goes on and I just nod, not trusting myself to say anything else.

There are a few moments of silence before he steps closer to me and clears his throat.

"I've started looking for rental properties too. I'm going to open up my own security consultant company in town."

"The place next door is about to open up for a new renter," I blurt out before I can think it through.

"Yeah, that might be nice. To be next door to the bookstore... and you," he says softly.

I look away from him, not sure what to say to that.

I can feel it. My anger toward him is starting to melt already.

I can tell that he's trying hard and part of me wants to give him a second chance but the other part of me is still worried.

I'm still hurt over how he just seemed to throw me aside for his big plan. He wants freedom, to be able to do what he wants, when he wants and a relationship with me is going to hinder those plans.

It's only a matter of time before he remembers that.

It also feels like it's only a matter of time before I give into this attraction between us and give him a second chance.

CHAPTER 9

SPENCER

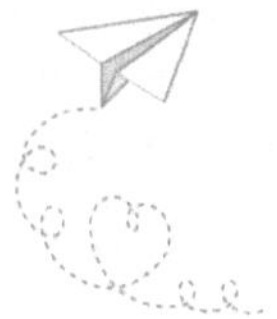

IT'S BEEN a week of me trying to show Emmy Lou that I'm sorry and that I'm not going anywhere. I broke down and asked Jonah, Zac, Drew, and Colt for advice one night over drinks. I had to apologize to them too for leaving so suddenly. They made me buy them drinks all night but that seemed to smooth things over. I'm lucky to have friends who are willing to forgive my stupid mistakes.

We spent the whole night brainstorming ideas of how to win her back. I have a handful of napkins with Zac's messy, barely legible handwriting on them. It was hard to make out all of what they said, but I got the gist.

Show her what she means to you.

Show her that you love her and are here to stay.

Grovel until she gives me a second chance.

I've been trying to follow that plan and to show her that I'm all in so I've been bringing her food every night and trying to talk to her. I've read every book that she ever mentioned to me and while I don't love all of them as much as she does, it was nice to discuss them with her.

I've been trying to help her out too. I mowed her lawn

one day, washed her car, and helped her stock some stuff around the bookstore.

I think that I've been slowly chipping away at her armor, but sometimes it's hard to tell with Emmy Lou.

I grabbed us some burgers from Lulu's Diner and I'm headed to the Book Addicts Bookstore for our nightly dinner. She hasn't invited me back to her house again and I know better than to push my luck with her.

It's starting to rain and I grab our food and hurry up to the front door. I spot Emmy Lou through the front window and like every other time, my breath stalls in my lungs.

She's still the most beautiful woman that I've ever laid eyes on.

"Hey," I call as I come in.

The front door slams shut with the wind and rain behind me.

"It's really coming down out there, huh?" She asks as thunder cracks through the night.

"Yeah, it's pouring."

The weather reminds me of the first night that we met and I wonder if she remembers it too.

"I brought burgers," I say and I see her lick her lips.

My cock stirs in my pants but I push those thoughts away as I walk up to the counter.

"And I found a place to open Elite Security Consultants."

"Yeah? Where?"

"Right next door," I say with a big smile and I notice that Emmy Lou looks happy about my news too.

"When are you moving in?"

"Next week. I'm hoping to get everything set up so that I can open by the end of next month."

I slide her a burger, fries, and a milkshake and fill her in on my plans. She's a lot better at business than I am so I pick her brain on where to advertise that I'm hiring and the best place to order business cards and the like.

We clean up our trash and it's still storming outside. The sun has set and it's dark, just the streetlamps and passing cars allowing us to see outside.

"I got you something," I start, my palms growing damp as my heart rate picks up.

I've never been so nervous in my life. She looks up at me expectantly and I dig in my pocket, the small box brushing against my fingers.

I pull it out and hold it out to her, opening the lid.

"Is that an engagement ring?" She asks, her eyes wide.

"It's a promise ring," I lie.

I was trying to think of a way to show Emmy Lou how serious I am about her, about us, and I landed on an engagement ring but judging by her expression, we're not there yet.

"It sure looks like an engagement ring..."

I smile at her, trying to think of how to do this now that my original plan appears to have changed.

"I'm yours, Emmy Lou. I love you and I know that I messed up before but I promise I'm never going to make that mistake again. I need you in my life. I was trying to think of how to show you that I'm serious about us, about making up for what I did and how I left."

Emmy Lou has a sheen of tears in her eyes and I pause, wondering if I'm messing all of this up.

"I landed on a promise ring. It might not mean the same thing to you as it does to me, but I hope when you look at it, you'll remember my promise to be here for you always. I'll still be here if you decide you're ready for that ring to be an engagement ring. I love you, Emmy Lou. I need you. Will you be mine?"

"Yes," she croaks, clearing her throat as she nods.

I slip the ring onto her finger and scoop her up in my arms. I don't give a fuck right now if she's saying yes to giving me a chance or yes to marrying me as long as I have her in my arms and she's willing to let me prove myself to her.

She feels so good, so right, in my arms and I squeeze her tighter.

It's late, the rain cocooning us in among the books. She wraps her arms around my neck as our lips brush against each other and it feels like everything is right once more in my world.

"You know," she starts, her voice husky, "the couch is still in the back."

My cock strains against the fly of my jeans as I remember the last time that I took her on that very couch and I grin as she grabs my hand and leads me back to the couch where we crash down onto the cushions wrapped around each other.

As her hands move over mine, the diamond in her ring catches on the streetlamp and a sense of peace settles over me.

Emmy Lou was never in my plans but she's exactly what I need.

She's my happily ever after, my future.

My everything.

CHAPTER 10
EMMY LOU

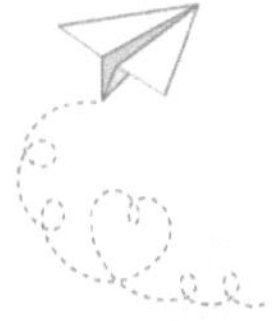

"I'll get that, baby," Spencer calls as I go to grab the box with the latest book shipment.

I didn't even hear him come into the bookstore but I should have known. I swear, ever since I got pregnant, it's like he has a six sense for when I'm about to lift anything over ten pounds.

"Thanks, honey," I call as he brushes past me, dropping a quick kiss on my lips before he hefts the box and carries it out to the shelf up front.

We got married a year ago and are supposed to be celebrating our anniversary tonight. Spencer made dinner reservations at Carantino's and I know that we must be running late if Spencer came in here to find me.

We just found out a few weeks ago that I'm pregnant with our first child. We find out in a month if we're having a boy or a girl and I can't wait. Spencer says that he doesn't care, as long as the baby and I are both healthy.

Spencer has his security consultant business all set up and it's doing great. He's right next door to the bookstore and it makes commuting easy.

We live in my childhood home and I had been worried that Spencer would have a hard time adjusting to a more stable life but he's taken to it like a fish to water. He loves being settled now and he's just as excited as I am to be growing our family.

"Are you ready to go, baby? I can come in early tomorrow and help you with the stocking," he says as he takes my hand and leads me to the front door.

He uses his own set of keys to lock up the shop as I tuck my cellphone into my purse. I stifle a yawn as Spencer tucks me under his arm and steers us over to his new car. He insisted on getting something safer than his Jeep and now we're the proud owner of a minivan.

"How are you feeling?" He asks as he buckles me up.

"Tired," I admit.

I'm still in the first trimester so I'm tired all of the time. Spencer is used to me dozing off now pretty much whenever I sit down.

"Do you want to just get takeout? We can go out to celebrate a different night," he offers but I shake my head.

"It's our anniversary. I want to celebrate with you tonight."

He gives me a kiss, cradling the back of my head before he heads around to the driver's side. As he slides in, I grin, reaching over and laying my hand on his thigh.

"Besides, I've got big plans for you tonight," I say with a wink and Spencer laughs, lacing his fingers with mine.

"Ben and Jerry's ice cream and falling asleep on the couch?"

I throw my head back and laugh as Spencer drives us to the restaurant.

"You know me too well."

"I love you, Emmy Lou."

"I love you too, Spencer. Happy anniversary."

"Happy anniversary," he says as he leans over and gives me a kiss.

I relax back into my seat, happy that the family tradition was right.

Spencer is my happily ever after, my Prince Charming.

I'm so glad that he walked into my bookstore that rainy day.

CHAPTER 11

SPENCER

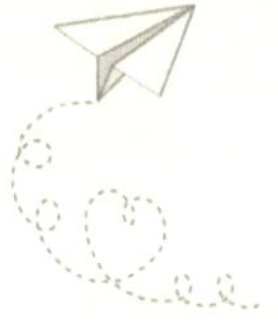

The plane rattles and Emmy Lou's grip on me tightens as we climb higher into the sky.

"This was a terrible idea," she mumbles over her shoulder to me as she looks around at all of the other pairs crammed into the plane with us.

The town below is so small and I can tell that she's having second thoughts. She's probably wondering how she can get out of doing this. I know that she knows that I won't make her do it if she really says that she doesn't want to. She's been so excited about doing it all week and I know that she just needs to get over the initial fear. Then she'll love it.

Emmy Lou and I have been married for the past ten years and we still live in Sunny Bend. I finally came clean and told her that the promise ring was really an engagement ring. I proposed for real and asked her to marry me a few weeks after I moved in with her and we've been together ever since.

She still owns the bookstore in town and my security company is still next door. Both of our businesses are doing good.

We reach altitude and I grin, turning to my wife.

"Are you ready?" I ask with a grin and she stares back at me wide eyed.

I'm finally taking her skydiving and I can see that while it had seemed like a good idea to her when we were on the ground, now that we're high up in the air, she's starting to have doubts.

"Our will is updated, right?" She asks me and I just laugh.

"We're going to be fine!" I yell back and she just gives me a dry look in return.

"Who did we leave the kids to?"

I roll my eyes and turn back to the plane door.

We have two kids, both boys and they keep us on our toes. They both wanted to come with us today but Emmy Lou had vetoed that one. I promised them that I would take them once they were older and I've been in the doghouse for a few days after that promise.

The plane door opens and I help her stand up before I shuffle both of us toward the door. My fingers brush over her wrist and I can feel Emmy Lou's heartbeat racing as she stares down at the ground way, way below us.

"We're going on the count of three! Got it?"

She gives me a shaky nod and I wrap my arm around her waist.

"One, Two, Three!" I yell and before she can blink, we're flying through the air.

The wind whips past us and I grin, although I'm sure

that Emmy Lou is too shocked to feel the same level of excitement that I do right now.

The parachute opens and we slow way down. Emmy Lou is strapped to the front of me so I can't see her expression, but she isn't screaming so that had to be a good sign.

"That was so cool," she yells a second later and I laugh at her excitement.

It's quiet, still, way up here and neither of us needs to raise our voice to be heard.

"Told you," I tell her smugly.

I let her hold the handles and steer us down lower before I take over again and move us to the landing area.

"Put your feet up," I order her and she hurries to do as I say.

We glide to the ground and I unbuckle us. Emmy Lou immediately turns and throws herself into my arms, laughing as I spin her around.

"That was awesome. Thanks for taking me," she says, pressing her lips against mine.

"Anytime."

"I love you, Spencer."

"I love you more, Emmy Lou," I whisper as my lips land on hers once more and I grin.

I know that I was sick of being sent all over in the Army and I was looking for my freedom but instead it's like I was dispatched to Sunny Bend to claim Emmy Lou's heart.

She is my freedom. My family.

She's my happily ever after.

My forever.